Henry's Bath

Margaret Perversi and Ron Brooks

PUFFIN BOOKS

Henry is going to have a bath today.
Oh, yes!

And a hairwash too...
In his own, special bath.

Well then, will we give the cat a bath?
No, the cat likes to wash himself.

The dog could do with a wash.
But it might get rather messy.

Would the hens want a bath
do you think?
Probably not.

The ducks might like a bath.
But we would have trouble
getting them out.

What about the goat?
I bet he needs a wash.

How about the cow, then?
Can she get in?

But Henry can hop in Henry's bath.
Of course he can.

It's warm
and bubbly
and ready to go.

Hey cat

Ho dog

Yay hens

Yo ducks

G'day goat

Howdy cow

Guess what?

And a hairwash too!